Don't Spill It Again, James

Dial Books for Young Readers

 NEW YORK

2663 10/93

Don't Spill It Again, James

Rosemary Wells

Library of Congress Cataloging in Publication Data
Wells, Rosemary.
Don't spill it again, James.
Summary: Three stories about James and his sometimes bossy,
sometimes tender, older brother.
[1. Brothers and sisters—Fiction. 2. Stories in rhyme] I. Title.
PZ8.3.W465Do   [E]   77-71513
ISBN 0-8037-2118-8
ISBN 0-8037-2119-6 lib. bdg.

Contents

Don't
Spill It Again,
James

What was that terrible crash
Just then?

There goes the ketchup,
You've done it again!

Why can't you look
Where you put your feet?

Watch that puddle
In the middle of the street!

Mother will blame it on me,
I guess.

James, you're an awful mess!

Everything's going to be
Hunky-dory.
Give me a kiss
And I'll tell you a story.

All about James
Who was three and a half.
He sat in a puddle
And he started to laugh.

He didn't know what
He was laughing about,

But he made the sun come out.

Skokie

We're on our way to Skokie.

Everything is Okey-Dokey.

I've got the money.
You've got the lunch.

We've got our presents
In a great big bunch.

We're on our way to Skokie.
Everything is very smoky.

You start to choke.
I start to wheeze.

Open up the window

And let's all freeze.

We're on our way to Skokie.

This train is very poky.

But never you mind.

Let's see a smile,

And we'll get to Skokie in style!

Goodnight, Sweet Prince

The owls and the crickets
Are singing together.

The clouds have all taken
The moon for a ride.

The first rain of summer
Is bending the heather

As soft as a feather,

I hear it outside.

Hush now, you hoot owl
And crickets be wary,

The morning is hiding
Behind the next cloud.

Let the sounds of the evening
Be pleasant and airy,

Let nothing be scary

And nothing be loud.